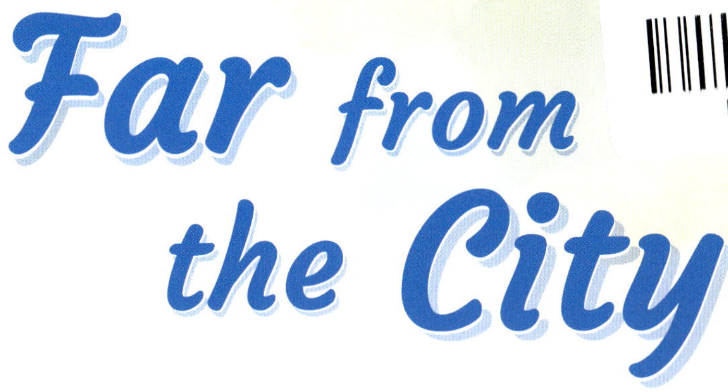

Far from the City

Heather Hammonds

Contents

Far from the City

Remote Places

Remote places are a very long way from the cities and towns where most people live. They can be found all around the world – in hot, dry lands or cold, snowy areas. There are remote places deep in rainforests and out at sea, too.

There is one remote place where people live and work that is beyond our planet Earth. It is the International Space Station, in space!

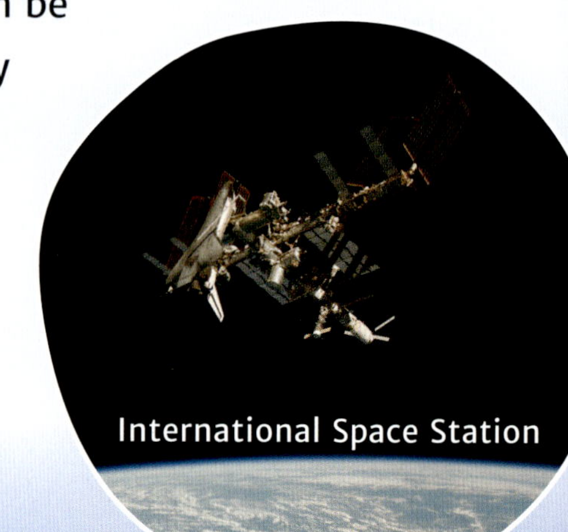
International Space Station

People live in remote places for many different reasons. They may have lived in a remote place all their lives or they may have moved there to do a job. People may also move to a remote place because they enjoy the **lifestyle** there.

Tourists often visit remote places that are beautiful or unusual, to learn more about them.

Beautiful remote places are popular with tourists.

Island Life

Living on a remote island has special challenges. Residents must take a boat or a plane if they wish to leave their island home!

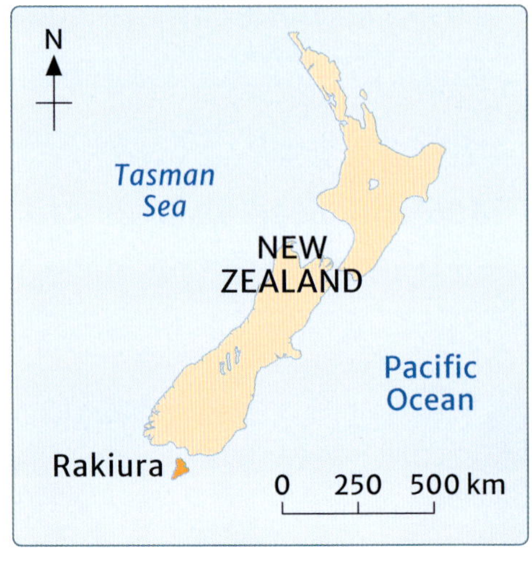

Rakiura

Rakiura (pronounced *rak-ee-oo-ra*) is a large island off the coast of New Zealand's south island. It is also known as Stewart Island. Most of the island is a huge national park. It is home to many amazing birds and animals. Kiwis, penguins and seals can be found on Rakiura.

Rakiura means "Glowing Sky" in the language of the **Māori** people of the South Island of New Zealand.

Kiwis live in forested areas on Rakiura.

Around 400 people live on Rakiura, in the small town of Oban. They can travel to the New Zealand **mainland** by ferry.

Rakiura is a popular tourist destination. Many people who live on the island work in the tourism industry. They welcome visitors, and help them to enjoy their stay and learn more about Rakiura.

Rakiura is a popular destination for people who enjoy nature.

Fair Isle

Fair Isle is a small island off the northern coast of Scotland. It is the United Kingdom's most remote **inhabited** island.

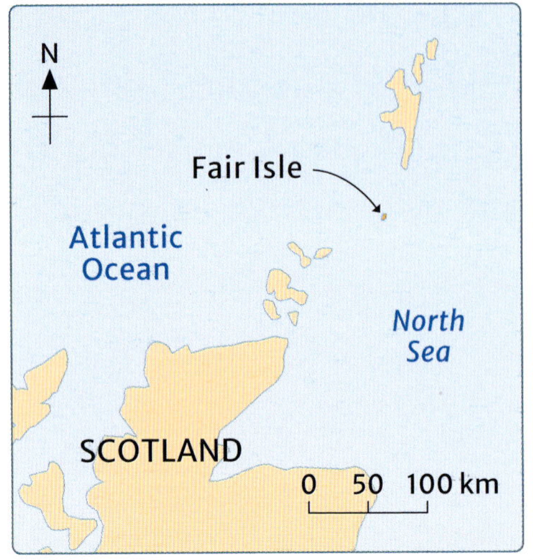

Fair Isle is an **isolated** place, with windy and cool weather. There are very few trees on much of the island, which has many steep cliffs and rocky beaches.

Fair Isle, off the coast of Scotland

Most residents of Fair Isle live on the southern part of the island. They work on small farms, called "crofts". They keep sheep for wool and meat. Other residents work on fishing boats or in the tourism industry.

The children of Fair Isle go to primary school on the island. When they are older, they must travel to a **boarding school** on a larger island about 40 kilometres away.

Sheep are raised on small farms across Fair Isle.

High in the Mountains

Remote villages can be found on some of the highest mountains on Earth.

Sikles

The small village of Sikles (pronounced *sik-less*) is found high in the mountains of Nepal. It is built on a steep mountainside and has views of the huge group of mountains called the Himalayas.

It takes several hours to reach Sikles from the closest city. Travellers must journey along narrow winding roads. Houses in the village are separated by lots of narrow stone pathways and stairs.

Sikles is home to the Gurung (pronounced *goo-rung*) people of Nepal.

Sikles, in the mountains of Nepal

The people of Sikles grow vegetables and raise farm animals on the steep mountain fields.

Sikles is known as a good place to stay for **trekkers** who explore the mountains of Nepal. Trekkers visit Sikles to see the village and the mountains around it. The people of Sikles welcome trekkers and other tourists to their village.

Villagers harvest crops on the steep fields in Sikles.

The Papua New Guinea Highlands

The Highlands are a mountainous area in the centre of Papua New Guinea. There are rainforests, grasslands and thick jungle in the Highlands.

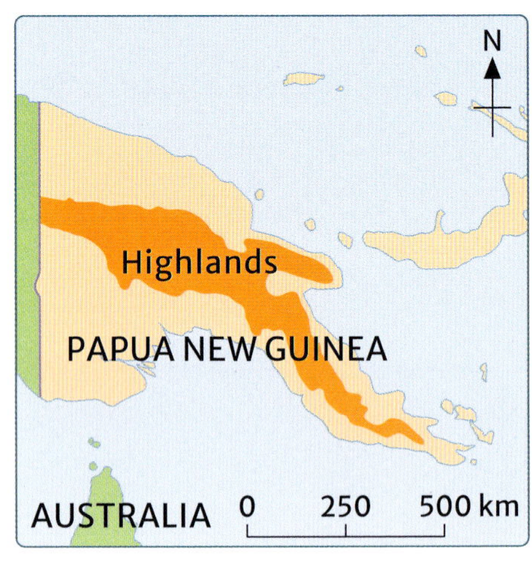

Many people live in remote villages in the Highlands. They often have very little contact with others outside their area. Their villages can be reached only by plane, helicopter or by hiking through the jungle for several days.

a remote Highlands village in Papua New Guinea

The remote village of Ambullua is close to Papua New Guinea's highest mountain, Mount Wilhelm. There are no roads to the village, but there is an airstrip for small aircraft to land on. Children in Ambullua go to the local village school.

Villagers welcome trekkers, who can stay in a guest house before visiting Mount Wilhelm.

remote fields near Mount Wilhelm in the Papua New Guinea Highlands

The Outback

Enormous, remote areas of inland Australia are called the "outback".

Outback Cattle Stations

Cattle are raised on huge stations in the outback.

Many cattle stations cover thousands of square kilometres. There are stations that are bigger than some countries. Because they are so far from towns, many have their own airstrip. Planes can bring mail, supplies and workers to the stations.

Life on an outback cattle station can be challenging. If someone is sick or injured, they sometimes need to be flown to a town or city for medical attention.

The Royal Flying Doctor Service transports sick people from remote places to a town or city for help.

an outback cattle station

Station owners or managers employ **station hands**. They do exciting jobs such as **mustering** cattle. Unlike workers on smaller farms, station hands sometimes travel long distances around the enormous cattle stations to do their work.

Many children who live on the stations don't go to an ordinary school. Instead, they do lessons online with an education program called "School of the Air". They use a computer to connect with the teacher and other children in their class.

Children from all over the outback attend School of the Air.

Cattle are rounded up by station hands on horseback.

Coober Pedy

Coober Pedy is a small, remote town in outback Australia. It is surrounded by bare, dry desert land. It takes more than eight hours to drive to Coober Pedy from Adelaide, the nearest big city.

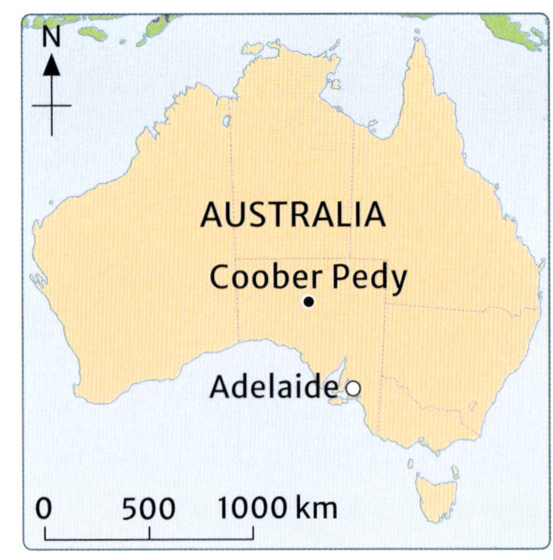

Coober Pedy is world-famous for its opal, a type of gemstone. Miners dig the opal from the many mines that surround the town.

The Kokatha First Nations people of Australia inhabited the land around Coober Pedy for thousands of years before miners came to dig for opal.

Coober Pedy

To avoid the intense heat, many people in Coober Pedy live in underground homes dug into the rock, called "dugouts". The rock helps to keep the indoor temperature the same, all year round.

Tourists come to the town to see the underground homes and the opal mines. They can also visit a mine or search for small pieces of opal in the mounds of sand, dirt and rock left behind by miners.

an opal

Rooms in dugouts are cool all year round.

Out at Sea

The ocean covers approximately 70 per cent of Earth's surface. Oceans can be remote and wild places.

Living on the Ocean

Some sailboats are specially built so that families can live on them permanently. These sailboats have a kitchen, called a "galley", and small cabins for bedrooms. They also have a bathroom, called a "head".

Families who live on sailboats sometimes sail across thousands of kilometres of ocean. They visit remote and beautiful places in different countries.

Some families live on a sailboat and explore the world by sea.

People who live on sailboats plan their travel from place to place carefully. They must take enough food and other supplies to last the journey. They must check the weather forecast, to see when it is best to sail.

Many children who live on sailboats are **homeschooled**. They do their lessons on board the sailboat. Laptops and other equipment can be powered from batteries charged by solar panels.

Electronic maps called "chartplotters" help sailors to work out where they are on the ocean and which direction to sail in.

Children do their school work aboard a sailboat.

Alone and Remote

Some adventurers sail their boats alone. Some even take up the challenge to sail right around the world by themselves. This is called "solo circumnavigation".

To sail around the world, people must cross some of the most remote and wild stretches of Earth's oceans. Solo circumnavigation can be very difficult, especially in rough seas!

It is challenging to live alone out on the ocean.

Solo sailors must do all the jobs on a sailboat when they are out on the ocean. These include keeping a check on their position, adjusting the sails and cooking their meals.

They also keep in touch with people on land and ships at sea. They use equipment that connects to satellites orbiting Earth to make phone calls and receive messages.

Solo sailors use mobile phones and satellite technology when they are out on the ocean.

Laura Dekker aboard her sailboat *Guppy*

In 2012, New Zealander Laura Dekker became the youngest person to sail around the world alone. She was 16 years old when she completed her journey.

Deep in the Wilderness

Many people choose to move far from the city to some of the wildest and most remote places on Earth!

The Alaskan Wilderness

Alaska is the northernmost state of the USA. There are lots of remote wilderness areas in Alaska, far from cities and towns.

Some people choose to move to Alaska and build their own **homestead** in the wilderness. They live **off-grid** and grow much of their own food.

Some people live in cabins in the remote wilderness of Alaska.

Living in the Alaskan wilderness can be hard work. There are many jobs to do around the homestead, such as helping to collect firewood and working in the vegetable garden. In winter, it can be extremely cold. Wild animals such as bears may live nearby.

The people who live there enjoy their way of life, far from the noise and busy pace of big cities.

a grizzly bear

People who live in the Alaskan wilderness often grow their own food.

Wilderness Houses

Houses in the remote wilderness are often quite different from houses in the city. They may be built from logs or other materials found in the area, such as stone.

Sometimes, people in wilderness areas purchase a "tiny house". These are *very* small houses, but they have bedrooms, a bathroom, a kitchen and a living area, just like larger houses. Tiny houses often have two storeys, with a bedroom upstairs.

Some tiny houses are towed into the wilderness, like caravans.

Tiny houses are popular in wilderness areas.

Unlike houses in cities and towns, houses in the wilderness are usually not connected to a public water and electricity supply. Instead, water tanks may provide a house in the wilderness with water. Solar panels or a wind generator may make electricity for use in the house. People build their house to suit the climate, so they can keep warm in winter and cool in summer.

Solar panels and wind generators make electricity for this house in Alaska.

Remote Research Stations

People live and work in some of the most **inhospitable** places on and around Earth, on stations built for scientific research.

Antarctica

Antarctica is the southernmost continent on Earth. It is a remote, frozen, windy continent that is home to many special plants and animals, on land and in the sea. No people live permanently in Antarctica.

an icebreaker ship

People and supplies travel to and from Antarctica on special **icebreaker** ships that can sail through ice-covered waters. Planes also bring people and supplies to Antarctica.

McMurdo Station, Antarctica

Scientists and **expeditioners** in Antarctica live and work on research stations for several weeks or months at a time. They take **field trips** out from the stations when the weather allows. They study things such as the effects of climate change on Earth, and Antarctic animals and marine life.

Satellites enable Antarctic expeditioners to keep in contact with the rest of the world by phone and internet.

Scientists study a colony of Emperor penguins in Antarctica.

The International Space Station

The International Space Station is a spacecraft and scientific base that orbits Earth.

This space station is so remote that the only way to travel to and from it is by flying there in another spacecraft!

Astronauts live and work on this remote base for several months at a time. They may stay there for six months, or even longer.

The International Space Station orbits Earth every 90 minutes.

Astronauts make repairs outside the International Space Station.

Each day, the crew may work on scientific experiments or do other jobs around the space station. Sometimes they leave the space station to test equipment or make repairs. This is called a "spacewalk".

There is no **gravity** on the space station. The crew must exercise each day, to help keep their bodies strong.

Astronauts on the International Space Station exercise for two hours every day.

Our world is amazing! We can learn a lot about it by visiting places that are far from the city, or by living and working in remote areas.

My Off-Grid Holiday

In the school holidays, I stayed with my Aunt Evie, Uncle Harry and cousin Willow. They've moved to a cabin in the mountains. It takes four hours to drive there, and there are no other cabins nearby.

At first, I was a little bit scared to travel so far away from the city. There were no shops close by. Did they have electricity out there in the mountains? I soon found out!

When I arrived, my cousin Willow showed me around.

The cabin is built from logs. It's off-grid, which means their electricity and water don't come from power and water companies outside. Instead, solar panels on the roof make their electricity. There's a wood stove for cooking and heating, and a rainwater tank for water.

Every day, Willow and I helped with the chores. We fed the chickens and collected the eggs. We helped milk the goats and weed the vegetable garden. Aunt Evie and Uncle Harry don't buy a lot of food, because they have their own supply of eggs, milk and vegetables.

Aunt Evie used to work as a teacher, and she homeschools Willow. During school time, Willow does some of her work on a computer, inside the cabin. The computer is connected to the internet. She is learning the same things that I learn at school.

Sometimes we went on hikes to a nearby river. It was very beautiful in the mountain forest. One day, we saw a deer!

I enjoyed my holiday in the mountains, far from the city. Living in a mountain cabin is fun, even if we were a long way from the shops.

Glossary

boarding school (*noun*) a school where children live as well as study

expeditioners (*noun*) scientists and other people who go on a journey with a particular purpose

field trips (*noun*) trips made by scientists and other people to study things they are learning about

gravity (*noun*) the force that pulls all things on Earth down towards its centre

homeschooled (*verb*) given schoolwork at home, rather than in a classroom

homestead (*noun*) the main house on a large farm

icebreaker (*noun*) a very strong ship built to break through sea ice

inhabited (*adjective*) lived in by people

inhospitable (*adjective*) difficult and uncomfortable for people to live in

isolated (*adjective*) far from other places and difficult to reach

lifestyle (*noun*) the way in which a person lives

mainland (*noun*) the main part of a continent rather than its islands

Māori (*noun*) the first peoples to live in New Zealand

mustering (*verb*) rounding up animals such as cattle or sheep

off-grid (*adjective*) not connected to public services such as electricity, water or gas

station hands (*noun*) people who work on outback cattle or sheep stations

trekkers (*noun*) people who go on long and difficult hikes

Index